The Cotton Candy Catastrophe
at the Texas State Fair

The Cotton Candy Catastrophe
at the Texas State Fair

By Dotti Enderle
Illustrated by Chuck Galey

PELICAN PUBLISHING COMPANY
Gretna 2008

*For all my carnival-going readers who stuff themselves with junk food
and nearly barf it up on the rides. Whee!
And a big, fat, Texas thank-you to Charles Trevino and Kathryn Lay.
—D. E.*

*To Forrest and Sean. Thanks for all your support!
—C. G.*

Copyright © 2004
By Dotti Enderle

Illustrations copyright © 2004
By Chuck Galey
All rights reserved

First printing, September 2004
Second printing, August 2008

*The word "Pelican" and the depiction of a pelican are trademarks
of Pelican Publishing Company, Inc., and are registered
in the U.S. Patent and Trademark Office.*

Library of Congress Cataloging-in-Publication Data

Enderle, Dotti, 1954-
  The cotton candy catastrophe at the Texas State Fair / by Dotti Enderle ; illustrated by Chuck Galey.
     p. cm.
  Summary: When Jake arrives at the fair, he heads straight for the cotton candy, but the machine gets stuck and Jake unknowingly trails pink, sticky strands behind him, eventually blanketing the entire fairgrounds.
  ISBN-13: 978-1-58980-189-9 (hardcover : alk. paper)
  [1. Candy—Fiction. 2. Fairs—Fiction. 3. Texas—Fiction. 4. Tall tales.] I. Galey, Chuck, ill. II. Title.

PZ7.E69645Co 2004
[E]—dc22

2003027660

Printed in Singapore
Published by Pelican Publishing Company, Inc.
1000 Burmaster Street, Gretna, Louisiana 70053

THE COTTON CANDY CATASTROPHE
AT THE TEXAS STATE FAIR

When Jake walked into the Texas State Fair, he passed up the funnel cakes, the popcorn, the nachos, and the corn dogs and headed straight to the cotton candy booth. He placed his money on the counter and grinned up at Miss Pearl Jackson, the lady twirling the pink, feathery confection. Miss Pearl grinned right back. But when Jake walked away with his treat, he didn't notice the long strand of cotton candy still attached to the spinning machine.

Miss Pearl saw what was happening and quickly flipped the power switch. The machine didn't stop. The tub kept spinning and spinning and filling up with cotton candy.

"Oh, my goodness," she cried, "this machine is stuck!"

The cotton candy grew larger and larger. It whirled like a Texas tornado, twisting and twirling and trapping Miss Pearl in a giant candy web.

The machine continued to spin out of control.
Cotton candy billowed over the side and slithered like a
rattlesnake, trailing on Jake's paper cone.

As he strolled by the carnival games, the barkers
yelling, "Step right up," stepped right in the icky mats
of cotton candy.

"What in tarnation is this?" one of them shouted.

They hopped onto their game counters, crashing pyramids of balls, darts, and stuffed animals. Everything fell with a clank and a clatter.

Jake never looked back.

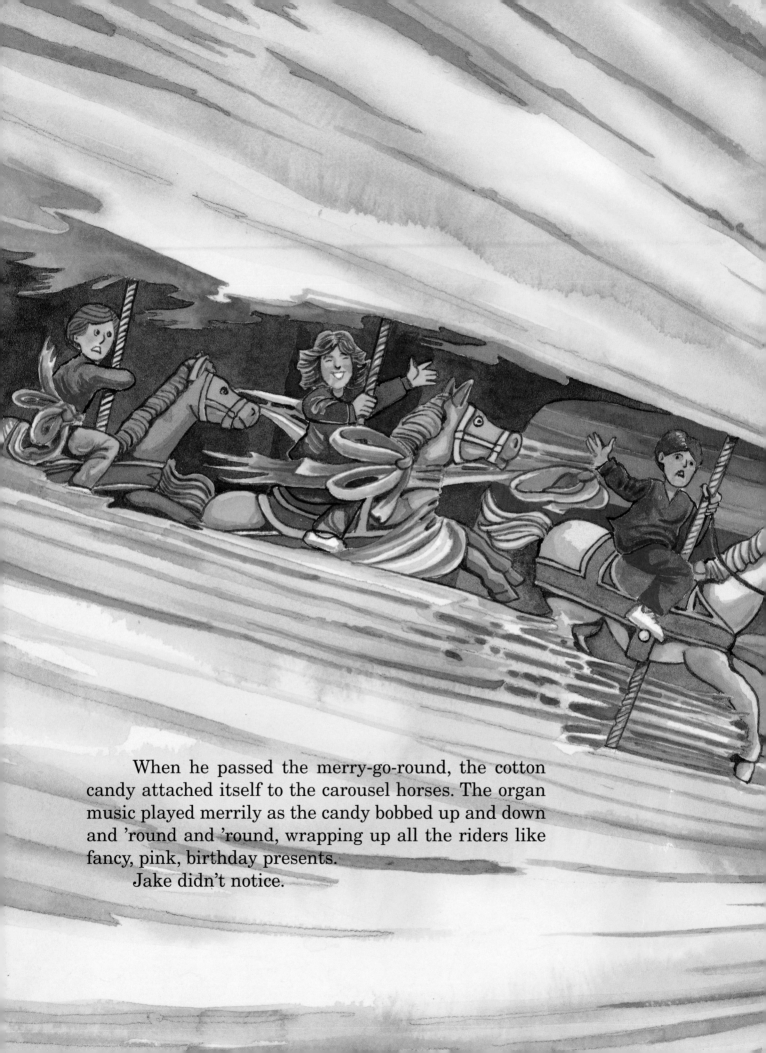

When he passed the merry-go-round, the cotton candy attached itself to the carousel horses. The organ music played merrily as the candy bobbed up and down and 'round and 'round, wrapping up all the riders like fancy, pink, birthday presents.

Jake didn't notice.

Midway through the midway, Jake came to his favorite attraction—the haunted house. He entered with the eerie feeling that something was sneaking behind him in the shadows. He clamped his eyes shut, took a deep breath, and bravely made his way through. Dracula, the Wolfman, and the Mummy, however, ran screeching and screaming as the cotton candy poofed out the windows, crawled down the sides, and crept along new paths.

Jake kept walking.

HERE LIES
COWBOY
RANDY

SEEMS HE
ATE TOO MUCH
COTTON CANDY

The cotton candy grew bigger and bigger. It rolled through the livestock pens like a tremendous tumbleweed, trapping the chickens, hogs, and Longhorn steer. Even the sheep wore pink wool.

Scarlett Scruggs, the fair queen, shouted, "Run for your lives!" Folks scattered. But when Scarlett tried to dash off, she tripped on her Miss State Fair ribbon.

Jake was unaware of the excitement behind him. Light bulbs shattered. Carnival music skidded to a halt. And it was just about then that Jake seated himself on the Texas Star, the largest Ferris wheel in America. The cotton candy hitched itself on too, and the Ferris wheel became an enormous spinning wheel, weaving a king-size cotton blanket that covered the park!

The Texas Star jolted to a stop with Jake on the very top. To his amazement, the entire park was wrapped in a sticky, cotton candy cocoon. People chomped and munched their way out. Others ran, grabbing their children and scrambling to the parking lot. Tires squealed. Horns honked. It was a nightmare.

But the worst sight of all was Big Tex, the fifty-two-foot-tall cowboy who greets the visitors as they arrive. He waved and shouted, "Howdy!" in a flouncy new pink tutu. What a disgrace!

Folks shouted for help.
"Call the police!"

"Call the fire department!"
"Call the Texas Rangers!"
But Jake had a better idea.
"Someone let me down!" he shouted.

A few men trudged forward and tugged the lever of the Texas Star, lowering Jake to the ground. And then, holding his paper cone high above his head, Jake found a trail unblazed by his cotton candy.

He led it in and out, curving this way and that until he came to the perfect place. Jake herded every bit of that cotton candy right into . . . the Cotton Bowl.

Firemen arrived and turned on their hoses, changing the monster cotton candy into puddles of sugar water. And with a wump, wump, wump, the machine ran out of cotton candy. Soon, it was business as usual at the Texas State Fair.

It suddenly occurred to Jake that he was still hungry.

"I think I'll have some taffy now!"